Published by Jeanette Kwakye
www.femithefox.net

Text copyright © Jeanette Kwakye
Illustrations copyright © Katlego Kgabale

First published 2017
ISBN - 978-1542550383

All rights reserved. Without limiting the rights under copyright reserved above, no part of this publication may be reproduced, stored in or introduced into a retrieval system, or transmitted in any form or by any means, without the prior written permission of the copyright owners.

This one is for the big kids, the little kids, my big man and my little man

Special thanks to, Grandma Rose, Samson Oni, Marvyn and Nina Harrison, Alec Boateng, Dipo and Alana Ajani, Cathy Francis, Annie Tagoe and Femi Oyeniran.

FEMI THE FOX
A POT OF JOLLOF

This book belongs to

_____

It was another hot day in the village and
Femi the Fox was hungry.
He was always hungry.

His tummy rumbled as he walked through
the market looking for food.

"Mmmm, I would love a hot
pot of Jollof rice"
he said to himself.

He walked past the stalls that were selling colourful clothes, pots and jewellery.

He saw the children eating bread and fruit, but no one would offer Femi some food.

"Ah Ah," cried Femi. "Why won't anyone give me something to eat? I'm so hungry."

Femi went to look for his friend, Sola the Squirrel.

"Hello Femi, how are you?" she asked.
"Sola, I am so hungry and no one in the market
will offer me anything to eat," he replied.

"That's because you are always causing trouble!" said Sola.

Suddenly, Femi had an idea. "Sola, I know what we can do," he cried. "Let's go and see Olu the Owl. He is wise! He will tell us where to find food!"

Sola shook her head, "Olu doesn't like to be disturbed in the daytime. Why don't you just wait?"

"I can't wait. Lets go!" said Femi, as he ran off into the village.

Olu the Owl was fast asleep
in his tree when Femi knocked on the door.

"I am not sure about this." whispered Sola,
but Femi knocked on the door even louder.

Olu finally opened the door.
"Femi, what do you want?" he shouted.

"I am so hungry and no one in the market
will feed me. Please help me find food!" begged Femi.

"No, I do not help trouble makers." said Olu.

"Please! I promise I will be good, if you help
Sola and I find some food!" cried Femi.

Olu told them that the Big Oba was having a party in his palace that afternoon, where there will be lots of food.

"Femi, if you are patient, the young Prince will bring food to the market. You should just wait!" said Olu.

"I can't wait. Let's go!" said Femi.

Before Olu could finish, Femi was running towards the palace.

Femi and Sola arrived at the palace.

They could smell the delicious food coming from the kitchen.

Everyone in the village knew that the Big Oba loved food and so did his son, Prince Kayode.

Femi and Sola had to be very careful
creeping around the palace,
otherwise they would end up in big trouble.

So they slowly crept past the Aunties and
headed towards the kitchen.

Femi and Sola could not believe their luck.

They saw sweet yams, stews,
plantains and a big pot of Jollof rice.

Femi's mouth was watering, Jollof rice was his favourite food.

"This isn't a good idea! What happens if we get caught?" Sola whispered.
"Don't worry, no one will see us!" said Femi.

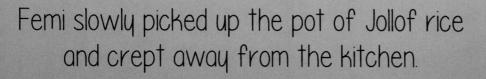

Femi slowly picked up the pot of Jollof rice
and crept away from the kitchen.

But, as soon as he turned the corner,
there stood Prince Kayode and
Chidi the Cat.

They had been caught red handed
stealing the Jollof rice.

Femi dropped the pot of Jollof rice all over
the floor in shock.

Sola hid behind him and Prince Kayode began to laugh.

"Why are you laughing?" asked Femi,
"Are you going to tell your Father?"

"No, I won't tell my Father!" said the Prince.
He could not stop laughing.

"Femi, why are you always getting yourself into trouble?"

Prince Kayode began to explain.
"The Jollof rice you have dropped was for
the animals in the market."

"I was going to bring the pot later. Now
look what you have done."

Femi covered his face with his hands.

"Now, none of the animals will be able to eat it. You should have just waited for me!" said the Prince.

"See Femi, Olu the Owl told you to wait for the Prince." said Sola.

Sola was very angry with Femi.
He was always getting her into trouble.

But, Prince Kayode had an idea.

"Femi, why don't you learn how to make Jollof rice?
I can give you an easy recipe to try.
Then you will never be hungry."

"It takes a bit of
patience and practice, but
I am sure Sola can help you!"
said the Prince.

Prince Kayode said, "My Father always tells me, 'good things come to those who wait'. I hope you learn a lesson from this Femi."

And with that, he gave Femi the Jollof rice recipe and went back to the palace with Chidi the Cat.

Femi sighed and began to walk back to the market.

He was still hungry.

Jollof Rice Recipe

Jollof rice is a popular dish in many African homes.
It's Femi the Fox's favourite dish and here is a special recipe for kids to try with an adult!

What you'll need:

4 medium fresh tomatoes
1 medium onion (chopped)
1 tablespoon of garlic puree
1 tablespoon of tomato paste
2 tablespoons of olive oil
500g of basmati rice (washed)
2 cubes of vegetable stock
1 teaspoon of ground black pepper
1 teaspoon of salt
Bunch of fresh thyme
1 responsible adult

With an adult, place the tomatoes in a blender for about 45 seconds. Make sure that everything is blended well.

In a medium sized pot, heat the olive oil on medium-high heat. Once the oil is hot, add the chopped onions and wait until they turn golden brown. Add the tomato paste, garlic puree and fry for 2-3 minutes.

Put the blended tomato mixture (save about ¼ cup and set aside) into the medium sized pot. Cook the mixture on medium heat for about 15 minutes. Make sure you keep on stirring the mixture so that it does not burn.

After 15 minutes, add the vegetable stock. Mix and add your seasonings (salt, pepper and thyme). Continue to boil this mixture for another 10 minutes.

Now its time to add the rice to the pot. Remember to wash it! Mix the rice very well with the mixture in the pot. You may have to add a little bit more water. Cook on medium to low heat for 20-30 minutes.

When the liquid has almost dried up, add the remaining tomato mixture. Cover with a lid, and let it cook for another 5-10 minutes. Heat until any left over liquid has completely dried up.

When dried, turn off the heat and mix thoroughly! Your Jollof Rice is ready to be eaten. It tastes great with plantain and salad!

Made in the USA
San Bernardino, CA
16 February 2020

64561291R00015